PUFFIN BOOKS

Lost and Found

When Lucy's family moves to a new town just before school begins, Lucy is lonely and worried about whether she'll make new friends. Then she meets a little dog that is friendly and may — or may not — be a stray. Her parents let her keep him until they find the owner, but Lucy, who calls him Trouble, begins to hope he has no owner.

When she meets Nan, a girl who likes to play detective, they set out together on the search for Trouble's owners, going door to door and scanning the newspaper "Lost" columns.

At first, Lucy is sure that no one could love Trouble as much as she does. But she begins to wonder when he shows signs of being lonely. In the end, she must make a choice about what is best for Trouble — and it won't be easy.

Lost and Found
Jean Little

Puffin Books

PUFFIN BOOKS

Published by the Penguin Group
Penguin Books Ltd, 27 Wrights Lane, London W8 5TZ, England
Penguin Books USA Inc., 375 Hudson Street, New York, New York 10014, USA
Penguin Books Australia Ltd, Ringwood, Victoria, Australia
Penguin Books Canada Ltd, 10 Alcorn Avenue, Toronto, Ontario, Canada M4V 3B2
Penguin Books (NZ) Ltd, 182–190 Wairau Road, Auckland 10, New Zealand

Penguin Books Ltd, Registered Offices: Harmondsworth, Middlesex, England

First published by Penguin Books Canada Limited, 1985
Published in Puffin Books 1986
10 9 8

Copyright © Jean Little, 1985
Illustrations Copyright © Leoung O'Young, 1985
All rights reserved

Printed in England by Clays Ltd, St Ives plc

Canadian Cataloguing in Publication Data

Little, Jean, 1932-
    Lost and found

ISBN 0-14-031997-2

I. Title.

PS8523.I87L67 1986   jC813'.54   C85-098643-5
PZ7.L57Lo 986

For Aunt Gretta with love from
Posy (Trouble) and Missy and me

Acknowledgements

I want to thank the Canada Council and the Ontario Arts Council, who helped to support me during the years when I was afraid I would never write another book. It was only with their funding and faith that I was able to finish both *Mama's Going to Buy You a Mockingbird* and *Lost and Found*. I would also like to thank Ellen S. Rudin who first suggested that I try to write a novel for younger children. Because of her, *Lost and Found* became a book.

Contents

Lost and
Found

One
No Friends

Lucy Bell felt lost. She stood at the window of the Bells' new house and looked up and down the street. She saw some little boys out playing, but they were not even old enough to go to school. She did not see one girl her size. She did not see any girls at all.

Lucy leaned her head against the glass. She blinked to keep the tears back. Then she took off her glasses and cleaned them on her T-shirt. She put them back on her nose and sighed.

"What's wrong, Lucy?" asked Mrs. Bell.

Lucy did not turn around. She did not want her mother to see how sad she was. But her voice shook.

"I wish we still lived in Guelph. I don't know anyone in this town. There's nothing to do here."

"There's a lot to do," her mother told her. "There are all these boxes to unpack. There are your books and toys to put away. I need someone to go to the store for me, too. I forgot to get ice cream."

Lucy made a face.

"I don't want work to do. And I don't like putting things away. I want someone to play with. At home I had lots of friends. But here I have none. I'll never make a friend here."

Her mother shook her head.

"Lucy Bell, that's just plain silly. We only got here yesterday. It takes time to make friends. Give the girls here a chance."

"I don't see any girls here," Lucy said.

Mrs. Bell was sitting on the floor sorting through a box of sheets and towels. She got up and went to stand beside Lucy. They looked out at the street.

"Maybe they're still on vacation," she said. "Don't forget that this is the last long weekend of the summer. But school will start bright and early on Tuesday morning. They'll all be back in time for that."

She smiled down at Lucy, but Lucy did not

feel like smiling. Her mother gave her shoulder a gentle shake.

"Don't worry. You'll soon have a friend. Now, how about helping me put things away?"

"I hate unpacking," said Lucy. "I'd rather go and get the ice cream."

"Well, let me make a list," Mrs. Bell said. "We do need some other things. Who knows? Maybe you'll find a friend on your way to the store."

Lucy felt happier as soon as she stepped outside. It was a sunny September day. There were no clouds in the blue sky. A warm wind ruffled her short red curls.

As she walked along, she looked for children her age. She saw a man cutting grass. She saw a woman shaking a mop out her back door. She did not see any girls or boys. But, three houses away from her own, she spotted a big tree with a swing on it. It was not a baby swing with arms. It was an old car tire hanging from a rope.

Lucy stopped walking. She looked at the yellow house that went with the swing. Nobody was at any of the windows. Quickly and quietly Lucy went over to the tree. She slipped into the tire and tried it out. Her feet just reached the ground. The child who owned the swing must be close to her size.

Lucy slid out of the tire and ran back to the sidewalk. The boy or girl who lived in that house might be home later today.

I hope it's a girl, Lucy said to herself.

She went on down Maple Road toward the store. It was very quiet. The only sound she could hear was the noise made by her own feet. No radios played. No dogs barked. No babies cried. It was as though everyone were under a spell like the people in Sleeping Beauty.

If only Kathy were here, Lucy thought, we could play at Sleeping Beauty.

Lucy missed Kathy most of all. Kathy had lived next door to her in Guelph. The two of them had been friends since kindergarten. Lucy gulped. She did not want to think about Kathy right now. She hurried into the store.

The store inside was a lot like the corner store in Guelph. A lady carrying a baby and a big bag of groceries was on her way out. Lucy held the door open for her. The lady gave her a big smile.

"Thanks, honey," she said.

Lucy smiled back. Then she began to look for the things on her list. She had to ask for the milk. The man behind the counter did not seem to notice she was new here. A lot of kids must come to his store.

Lucy looked over the candy. Her mother had said she could spend a dime on herself. She chose some licorice. When she had paid for everything, she put the change into the pocket of her jeans. Then she took a big bite of the licorice.

It tasted every bit as good as the licorice in Guelph.

When she was about halfway home, Lucy saw a little white dog. He was running down a side street toward her.

He was a very small dog. He had fluffy white hair. His tail curled up over his back like a feathery plume. His ears were soft and floppy. Lucy had a hard time seeing his eyes, because they were half hidden behind a fringe of silky hair.

He made her think of a mop.

Yet from the very first moment she saw him, Lucy loved him.

Two
Are You Lost?

When she first saw the little dog, Lucy looked to see who was with him. The side street was empty. The dog was so small that she thought he must be only a pup. He looked far too little to be out alone.

Lucy stood still and watched him. He was going up the street ahead of her. Each time he came to a front walk, he turned in. He ran halfway up to each house. Then he stopped short. He gave a worried little bark. Then, each time, he turned back and ran on to the next walk.

He must be lost, Lucy said to herself.

She hurried to catch up with him. When she

did, she put down her bag of groceries. She went down on her knees. She held out her hand to the dog.

"Poor boy, are you lost?" she called to him softly. "Can't you find your home?"

The little dog stood still. He cocked his head to one side. He peered out at her from behind his shaggy fringe.

Lucy did not move.

"Here, boy," she coaxed. "I won't hurt you, boy."

She kept her hand held out to him. She stayed very still. She waited.

Slowly, so slowly, the little dog came to her waiting hand. He sniffed at her fingers. Lucy had never had a dog, but she knew how to make friends with one. She let him get to know her smell. Then she reached up and scratched behind his soft ears.

"You're a good boy," she told him. "Don't you belong here, either?"

The little dog was listening hard. Lucy went on talking.

"If you were mine, then neither of us would feel lost. I'd be your friend and you'd be mine."

The dog began to wag his tail. Then he got up on his hind legs and licked her chin.

Lucy thought she would burst. She put her

arms right around the dog and gave him a hug.

"I love you, too," she told him. "You don't have a collar on. Maybe you're a stray."

She sat back on her heels and looked at the dog. She wanted him to look thin and dirty, as though he needed a home. Instead he seemed well fed and clean. Still, he was very small. It would not be right to leave him here. She made up her mind.

"You'll have to come home with me. I can't leave you with nobody to look after you. You might get hit by a car. If you don't have a home, they might let me keep you."

She stood up and got the bag of groceries. Then, walking backwards, she started for home. The dog watched her, his head tilted a little. Then he ran after her.

Lucy turned around and ran. When she looked back, the little dog was at her heels.

Lucy ran on. She did not take time to look for girls her age. Even when she passed the house with the swing, she did not slow down. She did not see that this time, sitting on that swing, was a girl about her size. The girl saw Lucy. She stopped swinging. But Lucy and the little white dog flew past without noticing her.

Then they were in the Bells' front yard. The little dog was still right behind her. They went up onto the porch together.

"You wait here, boy," Lucy told him.

He looked up at her. Then he sat down to wait.

"You're so smart," Lucy said. "You understand every word I say."

He did not try to come in with her. She ran out to the kitchen and put the ice cream away. Then she hurried back to the front hall. Her mother was coming down the stairs. Lucy crossed her fingers.

"Guess what, Mum," she began.

"I can't guess. You tell me," her mother said.

"I've made a friend," Lucy told her. "You said I might find one on the way to the store. You were nearly right. I met him on the way home. He's outside right now."

"How nice!" Mrs. Bell said. "What's his name? Why didn't you bring him in?"

"He didn't tell me his name," Lucy laughed. "Come and meet him."

She opened the front door. Mrs. Bell looked out. There on the porch, right where Lucy had left him, sat the little white dog.

Three
Trouble

The small dog on the Bells' front porch looked up at Lucy's mother. He tipped his head a little to one side. His tail quivered for a moment and then wagged hard. Mrs. Bell smiled.

"Oh, Lucy, what a dear little dog! Whose dog is he?"

"He's a stray," Lucy said firmly. "He doesn't belong to anybody. Please, Mum, may I keep him?"

Lucy's mother stopped smiling at the dog. She looked at Lucy instead.

"Lucy, you know better than that. You don't just bring somebody else's dog home and keep him."

"But he was lost!" Lucy stood very straight. "I couldn't just leave him."

"If he really was lost, his people must be looking for him this minute." Mrs. Bell's eyes were kind but her voice was firm. "You must take him right back where you found him."

Lucy took a deep breath.

"Mum, I didn't find him standing in one place. He was lost, honest. He was running along the street and he was scared. I'm sure he doesn't have a home. Nobody wants him but me!"

Lucy felt like yelling all this at her mother. She tried not to but her voice did grow loud. It began to shake, too. The little dog looked from her face to her mother's. He gave a small whimper.

"Poor boy," Mrs. Bell said.

She leaned down to pat him. At once he put his front paw up as if he wanted to shake hands. Mrs. Bell laughed. Lucy stopped wanting to yell.

"See, Mum, he likes you," she said. "He wants to stay with us. And he's just a baby. We have to take care of him."

Mrs. Bell put her arm around Lucy.

"Use your eyes, Lucy Bell. This is not a dog with no home," she said softly. "He's well fed.

His coat is brushed. Someone has taken good care of him. I don't think he's just a puppy, either. He's a Maltese. They're toy dogs. They are very small even when they are fully grown. He's too well behaved to be only a baby." She frowned. "The one thing I can't understand is why he has no collar. A dog tag would help us to find his owner."

"Maybe his owner moved away and left him behind. Or maybe she's got another dog she loves better than him. She can't really love him. If she did, she wouldn't let him get lost."

Lucy's mother sighed. She stood back to let the little dog come into the house. Lucy's face grew bright with hope. Had her mum given in already?

Mrs. Bell had not.

"If nobody loved him, Lucy," she said, "he wouldn't be so friendly. Tell me the truth. Are you sure he was running loose? Did you coax him to follow you?"

Lucy looked down. She *had* called to him. But he *had* been running loose before she called. She was quite sure he did not belong where she had first seen him. She raised her chin. She faced her mother and told her the truth.

"He really was lost," she ended up.

"Well, he can stay until your father comes home, anyway. I have to get back to those boxes. Dad will be here soon. Then the three of us can talk it over. But don't get your hopes up, Lucy."

Mrs. Bell turned to go back up the stairs. Lucy did a little dance. The little dog wagged his tail. He jumped around her as if he were dancing, too.

"Can I give him something to eat?" she called to her mother.

"You can give him a drink of water. Put it in a bowl and leave it where he can help himself when he gets thirsty. But *do* try to remember that he has a good home and people who love him."

The little dog had a big drink of water. When he was done, Lucy ran up to her room. He followed her, just like the dogs on TV. She looked in her box of toys and found her bouncing ball. The two of them went back down to the living room. She could roll the ball for him there. He stood waiting to play, his eyes bright.

Lucy sat down on the floor and looked at him.

"I wish I knew your name. I wonder if I could guess it."

The little dog did not want her to guess his name. He wanted her to roll the ball. When she did, he tore after it. He ran back to her with the ball in his mouth. He put it into her hand.

"Oh, you're so smart," Lucy said. "I never saw such a smart dog."

He barked at her to roll the ball again. He fetched it ten times in a row. Then he sat down to rest.

Maybe now she could guess his name.

"Is your name Skipper?" she asked.

The little dog just sat there. She tried other names. Chum. Bingo. Snowy. Pal. Mopsy. Rumpelstiltskin. The dog lay down. He put his chin on his paws. None of those names was the right one. She would have to try again later.

A car door slammed. Her dad was home. Lucy sat very still and wished. She had a feeling that if she wished very, very hard, her father might say she could keep the little dog. Then she would not mind having no friends here in Riverside. He would be her friend.

She heard her father's step outside the living-room door. She heard his voice.

"Lucy, your mother says you want to talk to me. What's the trouble?"

The little white dog jumped up. He raced to Lucy's father. He wagged his tail hard. He gave a quick high bark. Lucy stared at him. He couldn't know her dad already.

Mr. Bell squatted down and held out his hand.

"You're the trouble, are you?" he said, smiling at the excited dog.

The small white dog bounced up and down with joy. He looked from Mr. Bell to Lucy as if he wanted them to understand.

Then Lucy thought maybe she did understand.

"Trouble," she called. "Here, Trouble. Here, Trouble."

The small dog spun around. He raced over to her, ears flying. He jumped up at her. He licked her face. He knocked her glasses crooked. Lucy began to laugh.

"Dad," she said, "meet my new friend. I think his name is Trouble."

Four

Dad Makes a Call

Lucy's father liked Trouble. He sat and patted the dog while Lucy told him how she had found him. But when she said that Trouble was a stray with no home, her father shook his head just as her mother had done.

"Someone loves him," he said. "What if he were your dog? Think how you'd feel if he got lost. We must do our best to find his people."

Lucy did not want to listen.

"His people must be mean," she said. "If they loved him, why did they call him Trouble? He's no trouble."

Trouble looked pleased at the sound of his name. Lucy's dad laughed.

"A puppy is a lot of trouble," he said. "When Trouble was a pup, I'm sure he lived up to his name."

He gave Trouble one more pat. Then he stood up.

"I'll call the animal shelter. I'm sure someone must have phoned in to say he was lost."

Lucy knew that the animal shelter was a place where people looked after animals that were lost or hurt. She wished she knew of a way to keep her dad from making the call. But she did not.

Mr. Bell went to the phone. Lucy and Trouble stood beside him while he found the number. They watched him make the call. Lucy crossed her fingers. She held her breath while her father told about Trouble.

"Let us know if someone does call," he said into the telephone. "We'll keep him until somebody comes for him."

Lucy let out her breath in a sigh. Then her dad, turning from the phone, saw the smile on her face.

"Lucy, get used to the idea," he said. "Someone will miss Trouble and want him back. I have to go out again later. I'll get a newspaper. Maybe there will be something about him in the Lost and Found section."

But Lucy could not help hoping. Trouble loved her and she loved him. She was sure he wanted to stay.

"Why don't you take him out for a walk?" Mr. Bell said. "I have some rope you can use for a leash."

Soon Lucy and Trouble were going down the front steps and along the sidewalk. This time, as she and Trouble came to the third house, Lucy looked over at the swing. Standing beside it was girl, a girl only a little taller than Lucy.

Five

Nan

Lucy stopped walking and stared at the girl by the swing. She was eating a cookie. As she went on eating, she looked at Lucy. She looked at Trouble, too.

"Is that your dog?" she asked.

Lucy did not know what to say. She saw that the girl had long, straight, fair hair and bright blue eyes. She did not look very friendly.

"I said, is that your dog?" the girl repeated.

Lucy wished the girl had asked her something else. She looked down at Trouble.

"He's sort of mine," she said in a low voice. Then she talked on quickly. "We just moved here yesterday. I live in the house with the blue door. My name is Lucy Bell. What's yours?"

The girl finished her cookie. She stared hard at Lucy.

"What do you mean he's sort of your dog?" she said slowly.

Lucy put her shoulders back. She pushed her glasses up on her nose. Her cheeks got red. So what if this girl was a bit taller than she was! Lucy had told what her name was. Now it was the other girl's turn.

"What's your name?" Lucy said again.

Suddenly the other girl smiled. Lucy liked her smile. Maybe she was nice after all.

"I'm Nan Greenwood," the girl said. "I saw you move in. You didn't have a dog yesterday."

Trouble pulled at the rope. He did not like to stand still. Lucy looked from him to Nan.

"I'm taking him for a walk," she said.

"I'll come, too," Nan said, as if Lucy had asked her. "Can I hold the rope?"

"No," Lucy said, her voice sharp. She thought fast. Then she added, "My dad says I have to hold it myself."

Nan looked surprised. Lucy was afraid she was going to ask why. But Nan had something else on her mind.

"Where did he come from?"

As they walked around the block, Lucy told her the whole story. Nan got excited right away.

"You mean he's a mystery? I love mysteries! I read mystery books all the time. I'm going to be a detective when I grow up. Maybe the dog belongs to some millionaire and he'll give you a big reward to get him back. I'll help you find out where he lives."

Nan's words came all in a rush. Lucy did not say anything. She did not want a big reward. She only wanted to keep Trouble.

Nan did not seem to notice how quiet Lucy was. She talked on.

"First we have to go back to the place where you found him and look for clues. We could question people, too. Let's go right now."

"I can't," Lucy said. "My mum said I could only go around the block. She needs me to help unpack. I'm supposed to go straight home."

Nan looked disappointed. Then she had another idea.

"I know something else we can do. We have yesterday's paper at home. Maybe somebody put something in the Lost and Found. It'll only take a second to look. Come *on!*"

Lucy ran in spite of herself. So did Trouble. Already Lucy could see that when Nan got an idea, it was hard to stop her. Lucy decided not to try. She might as well get it over with. If there was nothing in the paper about Trouble, she could tell Mum and Dad when she got home. Then they might give in and let her keep him.

"I'll bring the paper out here," Nan said when they reached the yellow house. "My mum's afraid of dogs."

She ran into the house. When she came back, the two girls spread the paper out on the grass. The Lost and Found ads were at the back. When they found them, Nan gave Lucy a little push to one side.

"I'll read them out," she said.

Lucy stiffened.

"It's my paper," Nan said.

Lucy was angry. Who made Nan the boss? She could go home and read her own paper. She started to get up. Nan caught hold of her arm.

"We'll take turns reading," she said quickly. "You can go first if you want to."

Lucy sat back down. She looked at Nan's face. Nan did seem sorry.

"No, you go first," Lucy told her. "You're the one who wants to be a detective."

Nan bent over the paper.

"LOST ONE TABBY CAT NAMED COCO," she read out.

Then she got excited.

"Hey, listen to this one," she cried, forgetting to give Lucy her turn.

"LOST," she read out, "ONE SMALL WHITE PUPPY . . ."

Lucy sat bolt upright and stared at Nan. Nan rushed on.

" . . . WEST HIGHLAND WHITE TERRIER BREED, MAY ANSWER TO SKIPPY."

Lucy sighed with relief. Nan paid no attention to this. She turned to where Trouble lay, his head on his paws. "Skippy," she called to him. "Skippy."

Trouble looked up at her from under his fringe without lifting his head.

"His name is Trouble," Lucy told her, "and he's a Maltese, not a West Highland White. My friend Kathy in Guelph has a Westie. They're a lot bigger than Trouble."

"It says that they'll give a reward," Nan said sadly. "Are you sure?"

Lucy nodded.

"It's my turn to read one," she said.

Nan looked from the paper to Lucy. Then she said in a very small voice, "That's all there are. The others are all found, not lost."

Lucy was so pleased, she did not care about missing her turn. She jumped to her feet.

"I have to go," she said. "Come on, Trouble. Mum needs us."

Trouble and Lucy ran across the grass.

"See you later, Nan," Lucy called back over her shoulder.

Nan dropped the paper. She jumped up, too, and began to run after them.

"Tell me where you found him," she shouted. "I can go and look for clues there by myself."

Lucy heard her but she did not turn her head. She and Trouble ran faster. Why did Nan want to be a detective, anyway? Well, she would have to think of some way to keep Nan from asking people about a lost Maltese named Trouble.

Because Trouble wanted to belong to her, Lucy Bell. She was absolutely sure about that.

Six

Trouble's New Home

Lucy and Trouble ran all the way home from Nan's. When they got to the Bells' house, Lucy leaned against the front door. She was out of breath. Trouble's tongue hung out like a red ribbon. He looked as if he were laughing.

"We'd better go in and help Mum," Lucy said. "I told Nan we had to. If we do it, it will be almost true."

Trouble wagged his tail. They went in together.

Lucy and Trouble found Mrs. Bell in Lucy's room putting away her things.

"We came home to help," Lucy said.

"Good. I need all the help I can get," Mrs.

Bell said. Then she looked at Lucy. "I saw you go by the house a few minutes ago with a girl your age. Have you found a friend after all?"

Lucy put her red knee socks in the top dresser drawer. Was Nan going to be her friend? She was not sure.

"Her name is Nan Greenwood," she said at last. "She lives in that yellow house three doors up the street. She wants to be a detective when she grows up."

"A detective!" Lucy's mother sounded surprised.

Mrs. Bell left Lucy and Trouble to finish unpacking. When the things were in their right places, Lucy went downstairs and began to make a bed for Trouble. She got a heavy cardboard carton with no top. Mrs. Bell helped Lucy cut the side out with the butcher knife.

"Can I have something to put in the bottom to make it soft?" Lucy asked.

Her mother thought for a moment. Then she got some old towels she had used in packing. Lucy folded them so they just fit inside the bottom of the box. Then she took it up to her room and put it next to her own bed. The minute the box was in place, Trouble climbed into it. He turned around in a circle a couple of times. Then he lay down, all curled up in a ball. He looked up at Lucy.

"Mum," Lucy called, "come up and see something."

Her mother and father both came. When Mr. Bell saw Trouble lying there, he smiled. Then he looked at Lucy's happy face. He stopped smiling. He spoke to her firmly.

"Lucy, don't get your heart set on keeping Trouble. I'm sure that dog has a good home. Remember, Lucy, Trouble is not yours."

Lucy did not know what to say. Why did they all want to take Trouble away from her? If he had such a good home, how had he got lost?

The phone rang. Lucy remembered the animal shelter. She bent down and put one hand on Trouble's head. She listened.

It was only Grandma. Lucy let out the breath she had been holding. She did not think any more about what Dad had said about not counting on keeping Trouble.

When she heard her mother hang up, she went down to ask if she could go and buy a can of dog food.

"Please, Mum," she said. "Please."

"But, Lucy . . . oh, well, all right. Just one tin, though."

Lucy and Trouble went out the back door. Lucy did not want to go past Nan's house. She felt sure that Nan would jump out at her and shout that she had found Trouble's real home.

Lucy looked over all the cans of dog food. She wished she knew which one the little dog liked best. At last she picked beef stew. She wanted to buy dog biscuits, too, but her mother had said she could just buy one tin of dog food. Then Lucy had an idea. She put back the small tin of beef stew and took down the large economy size instead. That would be enough to feed a little dog like Trouble for days and days.

"I'll get you the biscuits next time," she promised him.

When Lucy and Trouble got home, they met Mr. Bell in the hall.

"I want you to come with me, Lucy, to show me where you first saw Trouble. We can try asking people who live around there if they know him."

Lucy's heart sank. What if she said she could not remember? She took a quick look at her father's face. It would be no use. He would know it was not true.

Her mother came over and put her arm lightly around Lucy's shoulders.

"I need a rest from boxes," she said. "I'll come along for the ride."

Lucy could not say a word. She had too big a

lump in her throat. Her feet dragged as she and the small white dog followed her father and mother out the door.

Seven

Nan Again

As the Bells and Trouble came out of the house, Lucy was so worried about losing the little dog that she did not notice the world around her. She jumped with surprise when a voice said loudly and clearly, "Hi, Lucy."

It was Nan. She was standing right next to Lucy's front walk. She was a little out of breath, as if she had come running the moment she had heard the Bells' door open.

"Hi," Lucy answered.

"Where are you going?" Nan asked.

Lucy wanted to tell her that was none of her business. It was bad enough that she had to go and ask people if they knew Trouble without having to tell Nan all about it first. Yet Nan's bright blue eyes were full of questions. And Nan was the only girl she had met here in Riverside. If Lucy had to give Trouble up, she was going to be more lost and lonely than before. She would need somebody. She took a deep breath.

"Mum, Dad," she said, "this is Nan Greenwood."

She watched her father and mother smile at Nan. They thought she and Nan were friends already. They were glad she knew someone her own age. Grown-ups often got things like this wrong.

"You must be the girl who wants to be a detective," Mr. Bell said.

Nan surprised Lucy by looking shy all at once. But she nodded.

"Then you should come along with us," Lucy's father said. "We could use a detective. We're going to try to find out who owns this little dog."

"Neat!" Nan said. "Can I really come? Will you wait while I ask my mum?"

Lucy did not say a word. Nan sped off to the yellow house. She was back in no time.

As Mr. Bell started the engine, Lucy sat very

still with Trouble on her lap.

"Which way, Lucy?" her father asked.

Lucy cleared her throat. She told him. It was not far to where she had first seen Trouble. She pointed to the side street from which he had come. Her dad parked the car.

"We could have walked," he said. "Why didn't you tell us it was only three blocks?"

Lucy did not know what to say. She was glad when her father did not wait for an answer.

"Let's go," he said.

When they were all out on the sidewalk, he smiled at Nan.

"Keep your eyes open. You might spot a clue."

Lucy saw Nan grin back at him. She thought they both looked silly. Playing detective! How dumb. She wanted to kick them.

"Come on, Lucy, dear," her mother said softly. "Let's get it over with."

Lucy bent down and picked up Trouble. Her father was ringing the doorbell on the nearest house. Holding the little dog close, Lucy went to stand beside him.

"Would you like to ask the questions, Nan?" Mr. Bell said.

Lucy knew he was being nice because he thought Nan was her friend. Nan blushed a little. Her eyes sparkled with excitement.

"Sure," she said, "if you want me to."

Lucy said nothing. She did not feel friendly at all.

Eight

Is This Your Dog?

Mr. and Mrs. Bell, Nan and Lucy all stood looking at the house. It was a tall, thin house with long curtained windows. Trouble did not seem excited by it. Lucy's hopes rose.

An old man answered the door at last. He looked surprised when he saw four people and a dog on his doorstep.

"What can I do for you?" he asked.

"Go ahead," Mr. Bell said to Nan.

Nan pointed at Trouble.

"Is this your dog?" she said.

"That's no dog," the old man grinned. "That's a mop."

Nan blinked. Mr. and Mrs. Bell laughed.

Lucy held Trouble tight. She knew that he did look like a mop. She had thought so herself. Still, it was mean of the old man to say Trouble was not a dog. He thought it was funny, Lucy knew. It did not seem very funny to her.

Nan was not laughing, either. Her face was red.

If she were a real grown-up detective, he would not make fun of her, Lucy thought. Over the top of Trouble's head, she glared at the man.

"I'm sorry," the man said. "No, that isn't my dog. I don't have a dog. I have three cats instead."

"Thank you," Nan said without smiling. She turned to go.

"Does anyone on this street have a dog like this, do you know?" Mr. Bell asked. "My daughter found him running loose near here and we want to find his home."

The man shook his head.

"Tina Marsh is the only one on this street with a dog. She lives in that red brick house at the corner. She has two dogs but they are big ones. Nobody's home over there right now, though. I saw their car drive off an hour ago. But I can tell you she has no little dogs."

"Thanks a lot," Mr. Bell said.

The old man stood inside his screen door and watched them turn to go. Lucy was the last to leave. She stayed behind for a minute putting Trouble down so that he could walk.

"You want to keep him, don't you?" the man asked her softly.

He did not sound mean at all now. The others were far enough ahead not to hear what he said. Lucy nodded.

"Well, I hope you get your wish," said the old man. "He seems to be a nice little dog."

Lucy smiled.

"He is," she said. Then she and Trouble ran after the others.

They stood by the car. Mr. Bell looked at Nan.

"Now what shall we do?" he asked.

He spoke to her as if she were a grown-up. Lucy was glad. She liked the way her dad's words made Nan stand tall again.

"We should ask someone else," Nan said. "Maybe he doesn't know. Maybe he made a mistake."

"I don't think so," Mrs. Bell said. "I think he keeps an eye on his neighbours. He sounded very sure."

"It can't hurt to ask," Lucy's dad said.

They asked at two other houses. Nobody

knew Trouble. Nobody had ever seen him before. When they came to the red brick house at the corner, Nan stopped.

"If this Tina likes dogs, she might know."

"The first man said there was nobody home there," Mrs. Bell reminded her.

"I can try anyway," Nan said.

She ran up the steps and rang the doorbell. They all heard dogs barking inside. They sounded like very large dogs. Trouble did not seem to like the sound of them. He did his best to pull Lucy back to the car. Nobody came to the door.

"We've done what we can here," Lucy's father said. "Let's go home."

Mr. Bell dropped Nan off at the yellow house.

"See you tomorrow, Lucy," Nan said.

Lucy waved her free hand. The other one was around Trouble. Nan looked at him through the open car window.

"Don't you worry, boy," she said. "I'll think of some way to find your home for you. So long."

She turned and ran inside. Lucy's father drove on.

"Nan seems like a nice girl," he said to Lucy over his shoulder.

Lucy looked down at the little white dog who was snuggled close beside her. She wanted to tell her father that right now Nan Greenwood was nothing but a pest. She wanted to say she would only like Nan if Nan would stop playing detective. She wanted to ask how she could get it into Nan's head that Trouble had a home with the Bells.

But she knew better.

"I guess Nan's all right," she said.

Nine
Trouble Settles In

"Lucy, would you please set the table?" Mrs. Bell said. "We're going to have an easy supper. I'm making waffles."

Lucy smiled. She liked waffles best of all. Even though she still was worried, Lucy cheered up. She sang as she got out the forks and plates.

"Oh, where, oh, where has my little dog gone?" she sang. "Oh, where, oh, where can he be?"

The song made her think of a boy or girl who might be looking for Trouble. She stopped singing. She looked for Trouble herself. He was not anywhere in the dining room or kitchen.

She found him in the hall. He was standing beside the front door. He looked at her as if he wanted her to open it for him.

"You're not lost now, Trouble," Lucy told him. "You're here with me. Remember the bed I made for you? You're going to sleep in my room."

Trouble did not wag his tail. He did not come to her. He went on looking at the door. When she just stood there, he turned to her again. He gave one sharp bark.

"No, Trouble, no," Lucy whispered. "You're happy here. You want to stay."

She leaned over and picked him up. She carried him up the stairs to her room. She put him in his new bed.

"See, silly," she said. "That's where you're going to sleep."

The little dog stood there for a minute without moving. Then he sniffed all around inside the box. At last he lay down. But as soon as Lucy stepped back out of his way, Trouble jumped out of his nice bed and ran back down the stairs to stand by the front door.

Tears filled Lucy's eyes.

"Leave him be, Lucy," Mrs. Bell said. "He's not used to us yet. He'll be all right. Dad has checked the evening paper. There's nothing about a lost Maltese. So you can relax for a bit. Wash your hands for supper."

When the Bells sat down to eat, Trouble left the front door. He came straight to Lucy's chair. Then he sat up and begged. He liked waffles, too.

Lucy wanted to jump down and hug him. She broke off a bite of waffle for him instead.

"None of that, Lucy Bell," her father said. "He must learn right from the start that he can't have food from the table."

Lucy felt mean.

"I'm sorry, boy," she said to the little dog.

"Trouble, get *down!*" Lucy's mother said in a sharp voice.

Trouble looked so sad that Lucy's heart ached. But he knew what Mrs. Bell's words meant. He stopped begging. He lay down and put his chin on his paws.

Lucy ate her waffles. As she ate, she thought about what her father had said. She could not remember his exact words. But he had said something like "he must learn right now that he will not be fed from the table." That sounded as if he thought Trouble might be going to stay.

If nobody calls tomorrow, she told herself, he'll be mine for sure.

When bedtime came, Lucy's mother read two chapters of *Ramona the Pest* out loud. Trouble lay in his bed next to Lucy's and seemed to listen. He looked as if he felt at home. But when Lucy's mother turned off the light and went downstairs, he got out of the box three times and went to the closed door. He scratched on it with his paw. Each time, Lucy hopped up and carried him back.

"This is your bed, Trouble," she told him. "Stay."

At last the little dog gave up. He curled himself into a ball and fell asleep with a tired sigh.

Lucy lay awake a little longer. Was it really only this afternoon that she had found Trouble? It seemed years and years since she had stood looking out the front window, feeling lost.

Lucy rolled over on her stomach. She reached out to touch the top of Trouble's silky head. It felt warm and alive under her hand.

Ten
Nan Finds a Clue

Trouble woke Lucy in the morning. He jumped up on her bed. He climbed on top of her. He licked the end of her nose.

"Ooooof!" Lucy yelped. She pushed at him with both hands. "Get off me, you silly thing."

But she liked it, really. She sat up and hugged him. He wriggled free. He jumped down from the bed and ran to the door. He looked back at her and barked.

"I'm coming. Don't rush me," Lucy told him.

She reached for her glasses. Then she put on her clothes as fast as she could. Trouble barked again. She ran and got his rope. The two of them went for a run around the block.

As they passed the yellow house, Lucy looked for Nan. Was that her face at the upstairs window? Lucy waved and ran on.

"Your breakfast is ready and waiting," her father said as the two of them came in.

Lucy was eating her last bite of toast and honey when she heard a bang on the front door. Trouble barked and barked. He raced around in circles.

"Well, he's a good watchdog," Mr. Bell shouted over the noise. He went to the door. He was back in no time. Nan was right behind him.

"Look who I found on the doorstep," Mr. Bell said to Lucy with a smile.

Lucy had thought she did not want to see Nan this morning. But now she was glad after all. It was nice to know someone in Riverside. Maybe Nan would forget about looking for Trouble's home today. Maybe today Nan planned to be a doctor or a ballet dancer instead of a detective. Maybe they could play with their dolls.

But Nan had not changed. She had a piece of paper in her hand. She waved it in front of Lucy. Her blue eyes shone.

"I've found out!" Nan's words came in an

excited rush. "I heard it over the radio. I wrote down the numbers. Here they are. I thought of it in bed last night."

"Slow down, Nan," Mr. Bell told her. "You're going too fast for us. What did you think of in bed last night?"

Nan looked surprised. She went on more slowly.

"I remembered that they tell about lost pets on the radio. So this morning I listened. And I was right! This is the phone number they gave and this is the house number. His name is really Tippy."

Lucy stared at Nan's happy face. She did not understand what Nan was saying. Who was Tippy?

Mr. Bell looked at Lucy. Then he took Nan by the arm and turned her to face him.

"Are you saying you know the phone number of Trouble's owner?"

Nan nodded. She held out the paper for him to see. Mr. Bell took it from her. He glanced at Lucy again. Then he reached out and picked up the telephone. Lucy could hear him dial the number. The room was so quiet that she could hear the phone ringing far away. Then a voice spoke.

To Lucy's surprise, her dad did not say

anything. He hung up instead.

"Nan, you must have got the number wrong," he said. "They say there's no such number."

He looked at the slip of paper.

"Maybe I ought to try one more time. I may have made a mistake."

He tried again. The recorded voice still said there was no such number.

"Let's turn on the radio," Mrs. Bell said quickly. "They may give the number again and we can check it."

"The part about lost pets is over," Nan said in a low voice.

She stood first on one foot, then on the other. She twisted her hands behind her back.

"I thought I got the number right but I couldn't find a pencil," she admitted. "It only took me a minute but that must be why I got it wrong. I know the house number is right, though. It was easy to remember. It was 555 Bellwood Road."

Her face grew bright again. She looked at Mr. Bell.

"You see, it's your name and my name put together, sort of. We could go there and see, couldn't we?"

Lucy sat very still. She could not speak. She wanted to pick Trouble up and run and hide.

She saw her mother smile at Nan. "I can never find a pencil, either. John, why don't you take the girls and drive over to Bellwood Road? Do you know where it is, Nan?"

Nan looked proud of herself. "Yes. I can show you the way."

Lucy could not think why she had been glad to see Nan even for one moment.

Mr. Bell got Trouble's rope. The little dog jumped and danced around when he saw it. He was happy to be going out. Slowly Lucy got up off her chair. She took the rope from her father. She did not look at Nan.

"Come on, boy," she said. "Let's go for a drive."

Her back was very straight as she went out to the car.

Eleven
Tippy

Nan did know the way. Number 555 Bellwood Road was a grey stone house. Nan ran up the walk ahead of Lucy. She rang the bell.

Mr. Bell put his hands on Lucy's shoulders. They felt strong and steady. She wanted to lean back against him. She went on standing up straight.

"Chin up, Lucy," he said softly. "It'll soon be over."

The door opened. A teenage boy looked out through the screen. His hair was redder than Lucy's. He had lots more freckles, too.

"We brought your dog back," Nan told him.

"We found Tippy for you."

The boy looked at her. He seemed not to know what she meant. Then he laughed.

"That's not Tippy," he said, looking at Trouble. "We already found Tippy. She was right next door all the time."

He turned away and shouted back into the house.

"It's some people with a dog." Then he called, "Tip! Here, Tippy."

A dog came running. She was much bigger than Trouble. She was very fat. She had pointed ears and a long skinny tail. And she had black spots! The tip of her tail was black, too. She barked loudly at Trouble.

"The radio said she was white with black spots," the boy said to Nan. "What made you think that was her?"

Nan hung her head.

"I was getting a pencil," she said in a small voice. "I didn't hear the part about spots."

"Well, we're glad you found her," Mr. Bell said to the boy. His hand was on Nan's shoulder now.

Lucy led the way back to the car. She was so happy that she even forgave Nan. She felt sorry for her. She touched Nan's hand.

"Never mind," she said.

Nan raised her head. She began to smile again.

"From now on," she said, "I will keep a pencil with me at all times!"

Twelve
Friends

"Trouble and I are going over to Nan's, okay?" Lucy said when the lunch dishes were done.

"I thought you said Mrs. Greenwood doesn't like dogs. Maybe you should leave Trouble at home," Mrs. Bell said.

"Don't worry," Lucy said. "We can play outside. I can tie him up to their picnic table."

The phone rang. Lucy's heart beat fast. But it was only Nan.

"Bring your dolls," she said.

The girls sat at the picnic table. They dressed the dolls in their best clothes. Then they had a tea party. They used water for tea.

Mrs. Greenwood let Nan have some little cookies shaped like animals. Trouble loved them. He ate a lion, two elephants and a bear. When the food was gone, he lay down close to Lucy. It was warm and sunny. Soon he was asleep.

Suddenly Nan got tired of playing with dolls.

"Why don't we go and ask some more people if they know Trouble?" she said. "That girl Tina might be home now."

Lucy did not move. She had to make Nan understand. She spoke in a loud, clear voice.

"I don't want to ask anyone about him anymore. I want him to be mine. If he has a home, it must be a bad home. Good people wouldn't have let him get lost."

Nan stared at her. She opened her mouth to argue. Lucy stood up. She gave Nan a hard, straight look. This time she was not going to go along while Nan played detective.

Nan sighed.

"All right," she said. "Never mind . . . let's play Fish."

Lucy sat down again. She felt like dancing. Nan was not going to pester her any longer about looking for clues. They were going to play Fish instead.

Lucy loved playing Fish.

Nan went into the house and came back with a deck of cards. Lucy hoped the other girl would not ask her to shuffle. Shuffling was the one thing Lucy did not like about playing Fish. She was no good at it. Would Nan laugh at her if she dropped the cards?

For the first time, Lucy was glad that Nan was the kind of girl who did not like taking turns.

She watched Nan start to shuffle. Nan was not so good at it, either. She dropped some cards. She picked them up without a word. She tried to go faster. Then she dropped almost all of them.

"I can't shuffle very well," she said, her cheeks pink.

"Me, neither," Lucy told her. "Sometimes I drop every single one."

Nan looked much happier. She started to give the cards out. Then she stopped and looked across at Lucy.

"What if Trouble's people do come for him?" she asked. "Will your mother and father let you get another dog?"

"I don't want any other dog." Lucy's voice was sharp. She bent her head over the cards in her hands. "Have you any kings?"

Nan looked at the red curls on the top of Lucy's head.

"Fish!" she said.

They played for a long time. After three games of Fish, they played Snap and Concentration. Nan was faster so she won the game of Snap. But Lucy had a better memory. She beat Nan easily at Concentration.

"Barbara Christie is coming back from their cottage tomorrow," Nan said at last, putting the cards down.

"Who's Barbara Christie?"

"I thought I told you already. She's my best friend," Nan explained. "Her birthday is the day after Christmas. She lives next door to you in that double house. The Christies live in the ground floor apartment on the left side."

Lucy gathered up her cards and put them into a neat little pile. She did not look at Nan. She had hoped she was going to be Nan's best friend. Maybe this Barbara would be nice, though. Maybe the three of them could be friends.

Anyway, if Barbara doesn't like me, she told herself, I'll still have Trouble.

She stood up.

"Let's take Trouble for a walk," she said. "I'm sick of playing cards."

The three of them raced until they were out of breath. Nan told Lucy more about Barbara Christie then. She had a white mouse called Nosey. She and Nan were going into Mr. Good's class.

Lucy gave a little skip.

"I'm going to be in his class, too," she told Nan. "My mother got a letter."

She looked to see how Nan would feel about that.

"Neat," Nan said. "Barbara thinks we should start a club. Did I tell you that she wears glasses just like you?"

Lucy wanted to twirl around and around until she was dizzy. Instead she began to run again. The three of them raced back to Nan's house. Trouble won.

"Nan, come in and get washed. It's almost suppertime," Mrs. Greenwood called.

Lucy was surprised. She had thought suppertime was a long way off. She skipped home. Trouble bounced along beside her. She would not mind starting school the day after tomorrow. Nan and Barbara would walk with her. And they would start a club.

She opened the front door and went in. The phone was ringing. Her father answered it.

"We'll be right over," he said.

He hung up slowly. He looked at Lucy.

"That was the animal shelter," he said. "Trouble's people are there. I'm sorry, Lucy," He said. "I really am."

Thirteen
Andy

Mr. and Mrs. Bell, Lucy and Trouble drove to the animal shelter. Lucy was glad her mum was there. Tears ran down her face.

Lucy's glasses got misty. Her mother took them off. She put them in her handbag. Lucy cried on.

She had been so sure that Trouble was hers now.

She held Trouble close. He did not like her to cry. He wriggled free. He put his front paws on her shoulders. He licked some of the tears off her face.

"Lucy, dear, stop," her mother said gently. "Look at poor Trouble. He doesn't understand. He's worried."

Lucy gulped back a sob. Mrs. Bell took a handkerchief from her pocket and handed it to Lucy.

Mr. Bell was driving slowly, looking for the animal shelter. They came to a long, low building.

"I think this must be the place," Lucy's father said.

Lucy's mother got out of the car. She reached to take Trouble from Lucy. But Lucy would not let her have him. Somehow she got herself out with Trouble still clasped in her arms.

She started up the walk between her mother and father.

She had made up her mind. She was not going to give Trouble back to people who did not love him. She would not do it, no matter what anyone said.

I'll ask them how come they let him get lost, she thought. I'll ask them why they didn't call the animal shelter sooner. I'll ask them to sell him to us!

That would work! That was a great idea! If only she had thought of it sooner. Now it was too late to tell her father and mother. Her dad was already opening the glass door of the building. She followed her mother inside.

Lucy could not see clearly without her

glasses. The front office of the animal shelter seemed to be full of people. Had they all come about Trouble?

Then she heard a boy's voice.

"It *is*! It's Trouble! Oh, Trouble, I'm back. It's all right. I've found you!"

Then Lucy could not hold onto Trouble. He struggled to get loose. His tail whacked against her. He gave little yips of joy.

Lucy had to let him go. She saw the boy now. He was down on his knees. The minute she put Trouble down, he flew into the boy's arms.

Lucy did not want to believe it. But she had to. The Bells were not going to be able to buy Trouble. It was no use even asking. These people would not sell him.

Even Lucy could see that this boy and this dog loved each other.

Trouble barked like mad. The boy did not tell him to be quiet. The boy was not saying anything now. Lucy felt something touch her hand. Her mother was giving her back her glasses. She put them on and looked at the boy, seeing him clearly for the first time. Then she understood why he was not saying a word. He was crying.

Lucy stood and watched him. He was big.

Lucy thought he must be twelve or thirteen. Yet he was crying too hard to talk.

He doesn't even know we're here, she thought. The only one he sees is Trouble.

And Trouble only sees him, a voice inside her said.

Fourteen
Tina

"We only found out that Andy's dog was missing about an hour ago," the boy's father was saying to Mr. Bell. "We went to spend the weekend with my sister in Toronto. She has a cat with new kittens so we left Trouble behind. Andy didn't want to leave him in a kennel. He was sure the dog would be much happier with his friend Tina."

He stopped talking to look at a girl who was with them. Lucy looked at her, too. She remembered the old man telling them about a girl named Tina, Tina Marsh. That Tina had had two big dogs but no small one. Nan had rung her doorbell but only the dogs had been home.

The girl's eyes were red. But she was not crying now. She was looking at Andy and Trouble and she was smiling.

"I didn't mean to lose him," Tina said. She talked fast. Her voice was unsteady, as though any minute she might begin to cry again.

"My dogs, Nip and Tuck, needed a bath. I thought I would give Trouble a bath, too. It would be a surprise for Andy. I took off their collars. I thought I'd do the big dogs first."

Tina stopped to take a breath. She was looking straight at Lucy.

"It was a nice day so I left Tuck and Trouble out in the yard," she hurried on. "I didn't know there was a hole in the fence. It was such a little hole I didn't notice it. But when I went to get Tuck, Trouble was gone. I called and called him. I couldn't believe he was really lost. I looked everywhere in the house and yard first. I told myself he wouldn't run away, not from me. He likes me."

Lucy saw that all the grown-ups were feeling sorry for Tina. But Lucy was not sorry. She spoke up in a voice so loud it surprised even her.

"You didn't call the animal shelter. I found him yesterday afternoon. That's a long time ago. He could have been run over."

Her voice began to shake. Tina hung her head.

"I kept hoping I could find him somehow." Tina spoke in such a low voice that they had trouble hearing it. "I thought he would go home. Dogs in books always do. I really wanted to find him before Andy came back."

Andy's father patted her on the back.

"It's all right, Tina. He's found now. That's what counts."

Nan said we should talk to Tina, Lucy thought. She was right all along.

Then Andy's father looked at Mr. and Mrs. Bell.

"I'd like to give your daughter something for finding him and taking such good care of him," he said. "Andy thinks a lot of Trouble. You can see that. It was good of you to look after the dog till we showed up."

"Well, Lucy, what do you say to that?" her father asked.

Lucy looked at Trouble. He was so happy to see Andy that he had not once looked back at her.

"I don't want anything," she said. "It was . . . it . . ."

She was going to say that it had been fun looking after him, but she could not get the words out. She held her head up.

"Good-bye, Trouble," she whispered.

Then she had to get away. The front office was crowded with the Bells, Andy's parents, Tina, the man from the animal shelter. She looked around for a way out. Nearby was a door that stood open a little. Lucy ran through it. She found herself in a narrow, empty hallway. There were a couple of other doors, but they were shut. Lucy stood still and waited. Nobody followed her. She heard them beginning to talk again. She was safe.

Then Lucy leaned against the door, snatched off her glasses and let the tears come.

Fifteen
The Sad Dog

Lucy felt as though she were going to cry for a long time. She did not think she would be able to stop until she was at home. She did not want any supper. She just wanted to get into her own bed and cry herself to sleep.

As she thought of her room, she remembered Trouble's box. Sobs choked her.

Suddenly, from the other side of the door, she heard something go "Woof!"

Lucy gasped. That one bark was just the beginning. In two seconds it sounded as though every dog in Riverside was barking at her through the closed door.

Using both hands, Lucy rubbed away her

tears. She jammed her glasses back on. She eased the door open. Inside was a dimly lit room lined with cages. Most of them had animals in them.

They must be the lost or hurt ones that found shelter here.

Lucy leaned down and looked through the wire net on the front of the cage nearest to her. There were three small black puppies inside. They were all barking at her!

"Hush," Lucy said.

As if they understood her, they stopped barking and began to play. They chased each other around the box. They fell over their own feet. Two of them tried to box. The third one knocked the first two down and sat on their heads.

Lucy laughed. The tears dried on her cheeks.

She moved on to the next cage. She saw a mother cat with two tiny kittens. They were so small that their eyes were not open yet. Lucy watched the mother cat feed them.

She went on down the row. A few cages were empty. There were lots more kittens. She saw more pups, too. One white puppy made her think of Trouble.

She looked at the door leading to the front

office. Had Andy gone? She heard an outside door shut.

Lucy went back to watching the white puppy. He sat down suddenly. He yawned. He bit his tail. Then he went to sleep.

He would not know tricks the way Trouble did. Lucy thought of Trouble putting out his paw to shake hands, running and fetching her bouncing ball, sitting up and begging for a bite of waffle. Andy had taught Trouble so much.

Lucy swallowed and blinked away new tears.

"You're a nice pup," she said, putting her fingertips through the holes in the wire net. The puppy did not wake up.

Then she saw another dog.

It was a tiny dog, smaller than Trouble even. It looked like a fox cub. Its coat was a golden brown, like a fall leaf. It did not peer out from behind a fringe of hair like Trouble. It had a neat little head with perky ears. Lucy could see that the fur of its chest was soft and creamy white.

Yet none of this was what made it so different.

It lay very still. It would not look at her. It was staring at the wall of its cage. It had big, sad-looking eyes. Even though it was so small,

Lucy was sure this dog was not a puppy. Puppies were playful. Puppies did not look so lonely.

Lucy tapped the door of the cage softly. She tried to whistle. The puppies in the nearby cages yipped fiercely at her. The sad dog did not turn its head.

It made her think of Trouble waiting by the door, waiting to go home.

"Hello," she said in a soft voice. "Hello, little dog."

It looked at her then. For one moment it came alive with hope. Then it saw she was a stranger. It turned away. It grew limp again. It went back to staring at nothing.

"Well, Lucy, that's over," her father said behind her. "I was proud of you for not taking a reward. Your mother and I have been talking. We'll get you a new puppy tomorrow. You'll soon love it even more than Trouble. Now let's go home."

Lucy stayed where she was. She looked back down the row of cages. She saw all the puppies, big and little. They were cute. They were covered with baby fluff. Any one of them would be fun to have, fun to teach, fun to cuddle. The white one still made her think of Trouble.

Then she looked back at the small sad dog.

"Is this a lost dog?" she asked the animal shelter man. "Will someone be coming to take this little dog home?"

Sixteen
Missy

The three Bells were all looking at the sad dog now. The man from the animal shelter moved to stand next to Lucy.

"She's not lost," he said, "but she has no home. She's a toy Pomeranian. Poms they call them."

Mrs. Bell looked at the still little dog.

"Where did she come from?" she asked quietly.

"It's a sad story." The man was watching Lucy as he spoke. "She belonged to a little girl about the size of your daughter. The child loved the dog very much. Then her little brother grew to be allergic to dog hair. The doctor said they had to get rid of the dog. It was hard for the little girl. But she understood why. The dog doesn't."

He undid the latch on the front of the cage. He reached in and picked up the tiny dog. He held her against his big chest. He patted her. The dog lay very still in his arms. She did not look at anyone.

"She's five years old," the man told them. "She has lived in that home all her life. They couldn't find anyone to take her. I said that she wasn't lost. I was wrong. She's more lost than that boy's dog. They left her here a week ago and she's been like this ever since. I think she knows they aren't coming back."

"If she were happy, she'd be beautiful," Lucy's mother said. "She's so delicate."

"I think you're waiting for us to go so you can close this place up for the night," Mr. Bell said to the man.

The man did not answer. He was watching Lucy. Mr. Bell looked at her, too. Lucy looked only at the sad little dog.

"What will happen to her?" she asked.

"We'll try to find a home for her. Most people want puppies. But I'm sure someone will take her because she's an expensive dog. Whoever takes her will have to be kind and patient to win her heart."

Lucy stretched out her hands. She took the dog into them.

"I would be kind to her," she half whispered.

She cuddled the Pom close. She looked into the lonesome dark eyes. Very gently she stroked the red-gold fur.

"Why, Lucy, her hair is almost the same colour as yours," her mother said.

Lucy looked up at the man. He was smiling at her.

"Do you know her name?" she asked him.

"Missy, I think. He looked at a tag on the front of the cage. Lucy had not noticed it before.

"That's right. Missy," he told her.

"Lucy, that dog would never be all yours," said her father, breaking in. "We'll get you a Maltese puppy like Trouble. I'll get him first thing tomorrow. You don't want a dog with a broken heart."

Lucy stood looking at him. Was he right? Wouldn't a Maltese puppy be better?

Then Missy made up Lucy's mind. She did not lift her head to lick Lucy's cheek. She did not look happy. She just moved a tiny bit. She moved closer to Lucy. She pushed her head up under Lucy's chin. She rested it against Lucy's neck. She gave a small sigh.

Lucy ducked her head down so that she could speak into the dog's ear.

"Missy," she murmured, "oh, Missy."

Then she looked up at her mother and father. She saw her mother smile. She saw her father looking worried.

"Can Missy and I wait out in the car?" she asked them.

Neither Mr. nor Mrs. Bell said a word. They just nodded.

"Good girl," the man from the animal shelter said softly.

Lucy was not sure whether he meant Missy or herself. She did not stay to ask.

When she and Missy were by themselves in the car, she put her cheek down on the top of the dog's head.

"I'm lonely, too, Missy," she said almost in a whisper. "Trouble is gone. And I don't know if Nan and Barbara will be my friends. So I know how you feel. But it'll be all right. You and I will be friends with each other. After awhile, you won't be sad any more. Because you know what? I love you already, Missy."

At that, Missy's tail, which had hung so limply, curled up. And Lucy felt the tip of it wag ever so slightly against her bare arm.

Seventeen
The
Right Question

It was Monday afternoon. Nan and Lucy were out on the Bells' front porch. They were playing Fish again. Nan kept stopping to look at Missy.

"She's not much like Trouble," she said. "He was so friendly."

"I know," Lucy said.

She did not tell Nan that when she had wakened that morning, she had found Missy curled up beside her. She had not felt the dog jump up onto the bed. Trouble had never cuddled up close to her like that. She was tired of hearing that Missy was not like Trouble. Nan had said it three times so far.

"I want all your threes," Lucy said.

Nan gave her two cards.

"I wish Barbara would come home," Nan said then. "I thought they would be here by now."

Nan kept saying that over and over, too. Lucy sighed. It was hard to play Fish with Nan today. She kept talking about other things.

"Do you have any nines?" Lucy asked.

Nan did not answer.

"Nines," Lucy said again. "I want your nines."

Nan still did not answer. Lucy looked up. She saw Nan scramble to her feet. Her cards fell to the porch floor.

"Look! There's Barbara!" she shouted. "She's back!"

She dashed down the steps. She ran across the grass. Her long hair flew out behind her. She stopped beside a car full of people. A girl got out.

Missy had been lying near Lucy. Now she raced back and forth on the porch. She made little sounds deep in her throat. Lucy watched her. Missy had not barked once since they had brought her home. She had been too good. Too quiet. She had acted like company. Was she going to bark now?

"Hey, Barbara, I thought you'd never get here," Nan said in an excited voice.

And Missy began to bark. She yipped and yapped. She ran over and jumped up against Lucy who was still sitting cross-legged on the porch floor. She ran back to the top of the steps. She was watching Nan.

Lucy laughed. She got to her feet, too. She stooped and put a hand on Missy's back.

"Be quiet," she said. "Missy, quiet!"

Missy gave one more bark. Then she stood, ears forward, eyes bright, staring down at Nan and the new girl.

Lucy looked, too. Barbara was not as tall as Nan. She had short brown hair. Lucy could see her glasses.

Nan was bringing her over.

"This is Lucy, Lucy Bell," Nan said. "She's going to be in our class. I told her all about you."

The two girls were at the bottom of the porch steps. Lucy stood and looked down at them. Her face felt hot. She wished Nan had waited a little before bringing Barbara over. What was she supposed to say? She did her best to smile.

"Hi," she said. "Nan told me you were coming."

The words sounded dumb. Lucy wanted to run and hide. At last Barbara spoke.

"What a cute little dog!" she said. "Is it yours?"

Lucy remembered when Nan had asked her the same question. She had asked it about Trouble. It had been the wrong question to ask then. But now everything was different. Barbara's question was exactly right. Lucy felt happy clear down to her toes.

She leaned down. Gently she lifted Missy up into her arms. She smiled at Barbara over the top of the little dog's head.

"Yes," said Lucy Bell proudly. "Missy is mine."

Also by Jean Little...

Mama's Going to Buy You a Mockingbird

Jeremy is not having a good summer. His best friends have moved away, and he has to stay at the cottage with only his little sister Sarah and his Aunt Margery. His parents have remained in the city so his father can have an operation.

When Jeremy finally sees his father, he finds out that he has cancer and that he isn't going to get better. Suddenly everything is different. Jeremy must deal not only with his own grief but also that of his mother and his sister. He tries to be "good" all the time but it's hard — and then there's the gossip of his classmates, the sympathy of his teachers, and a move to a new, smaller house.

Jeremy finds an unlikely friend in Tess, who also knows what it's like to lose a parent. And as their friendship grows, through good times and bad, Jeremy discovers that his father has left him something that will live forever . . .